Harry's class were going to visit a farm.
"What animals will we see on the
farm?" asked their teacher, Mrs Brown,
as they got on the school minibus.

"We'll see lambs," said Lucy.
"We'll see ducklings," said Raj.
"We'll see piglets," said the twins,
Polly and Paul.

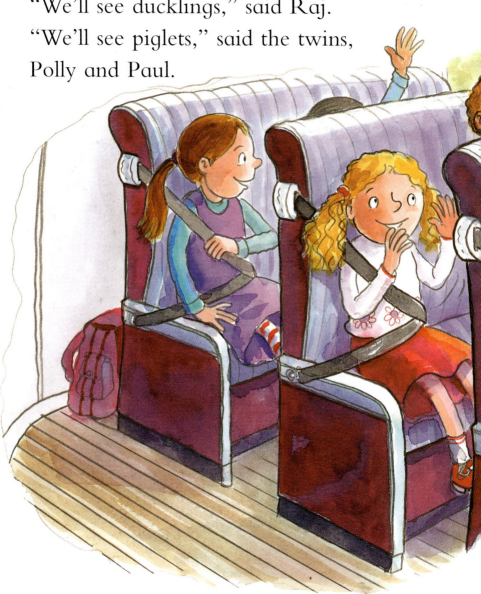

But Harry had other ideas.
"We'll see tigers," he said.

"Don't be silly, Harry," said Mrs
Brown. "Tigers don't live on farms."
Harry made a grumpy face.
He liked tigers.

"Now," went on Mrs Brown. "We know a song about a farm. Let's sing Old McDonald."

Lucy sang about lambs saying BAA BAA here and BAA BAA there, on Old McDonald's farm.

Raj sang about ducklings saying QUACK QUACK here and QUACK QUACK there, on Old McDonald's farm.

Polly and Paul sang about piglets saying
OINK OINK here and OINK OINK
there, on Old McDonald's farm.

But Harry sang about tigers saying
PURR PURR here and PURR PURR
there, on Old McDonald's farm.

"Don't be silly, Harry," said Mrs Brown. "Tigers don't purr."

Harry made another grumpy face. He liked tigers.

Soon they got to the farm. Lucy ran off to find the lambs. Raj ran off to find the ducklings. Polly and Paul ran off to find the piglets.

But Harry ran off to find the farmer.

He was in the big shed, mending the
tractor.
"Hello," said Harry. "Are you Old
McDonald, and do you have any tigers
on your farm?"

The farmer laughed and wiped his hands on an oily rag.

"I'm Farmer Jones," he said, "and it's funny you should ask about tigers. I do have some on the farm. Come and I'll show you."

Harry made a smiley face. He liked tigers.
Farmer Jones took him to the old barn,
and showed him the tigers.

"They're very small tigers," he said.
"You can stroke them if you like."
Harry stroked the tigers' soft fur.
Then he had an idea.

"Can I take one to surprise Mrs Brown?"
he asked.
"Certainly," said Farmer Jones.

When Harry found Mrs Brown she was
in the middle of the farmyard, in the
middle of all the children. They were
talking about what they liked best on
the farm.

"I liked the lambs best," said Lucy. "Especially when they skipped about saying, 'BAA BAA, where's my ma?'"

"I liked the ducklings best," said Raj. "Especially when they swam around saying, 'QUACK QUACK, where's my snack?'"

"We liked the piglets best," said Polly and Paul. "Especially when they trotted around saying, 'LOOK OUT, LOOK OUT, here comes my snout!' "

Then Harry said, "I liked the tigers best. Especially when they said, 'PURR PURR, stroke my fur.'"

"Don't be silly, Harry," sighed Mrs
Brown. "Tigers don't live on farms and
they don't purr."

"This one does," grinned Harry, and
out of his anorak he took a stripy kitten.

"Meet Tiger, everyone," he said. And
he stroked her fur and she purred and
purred.

"Well I never," laughed Mrs Brown.
"You weren't so silly after all, Harry."

Harry made a huge smiley face. He liked all kinds of tigers. Especially little ones!

30